THE EXTRAORDINARY FILES

DATE DUE

1 2 NOV 2012		1 3 NOV 2014	
2 9 NOV 2012		1 8 DEC 2014	
1 5 APR 2013		2 7 JAN 2019	
0 7 JUN 2013		2 4 APR 2017	
0 2 OCT 2013			
0 8 OCT 2013			
0 4 NOV 2013			
0 8 NOV 2013			
1 7 FEB 2014			
2 1 OCT 2014			
0 3 NOV 2014			

Demco, Inc. 38-293

'The truth is inside us.
It is the only place where it can hide.'

nasen

NASEN House, 4/5 Amber Business Village, Amber Close,
Amington, Tamworth, Staffordshire B77 4RP

Rising Stars UK Ltd.
22 Grafton Street, London W1S 4EX
www.risingstars-uk.com

Text © Rising Stars UK Ltd.
The right of Paul Blum to be identified as the author of this work has
been asserted by him in accordance with the Copyright, Design and
Patents Act 1988.

Published 2007

Cover design: Button plc
Illustrator: Enzo Troiano
Text design and typesetting: pentacor**big**
Publisher: Gill Budgell
Editor: Maoliosa Kelly
Editorial consultants: Lorraine Petersen and Cliff Moon

British Library Cataloguing in Publication Data.
A CIP record for this book is available from the British Library.

ISBN: 978-1-84680-250-8

Printed by Craft Print International Limited, Singapore

CHAPTER ONE

Peckham, London

Jack looked back again. He looked up and down the street but there was nothing.

He walked more quickly. He was sure that he was being followed. Jack was ten minutes from school and three minutes from home. He looked back again. No doubt about it, three teenagers with their hoods up were following him. He began to run.

The hoodies ran after
him. Jack ran down
an alleyway at the
side of a block of flats.
He didn't know where
he was going.
He ran until he had
to stop. The alleyway
was a dead end. There
was nothing but a row
of metal dustbins in it.
He turned to face
the three hoodies.
Might as well get it
over with. He hoped
that they would just
take his mobile phone
and not hurt him.

Jack could hear his heart thumping and his own heavy breathing. The three teenagers were on top of him. He tried to look at their faces but he couldn't see them. Then everything went black. When Jack woke up, he was lying in one of the dustbins. He felt his head. There was no blood. He still had his mobile phone.

Jack climbed out of the bin. He started to walk home.
People were staring at him. Some of them pointed
and laughed. Jack wondered why. Then he passed a
shop window and saw his reflection. He stopped and
stared. He couldn't believe what he saw!

CHAPTER TWO

Laura Turnbull and Robert Parker were British Secret Service agents. They worked for MI5. They were sitting outside the headteacher's office in a big secondary school in London.

"I feel like I'm back at school," said Turnbull. "I was always getting into trouble for fighting."

"I was always in the nurse's office, getting first aid," said Parker.

"Why was that?" she asked.

"I was always being beaten up," he replied.

At that moment, the headteacher came out to greet them. She looked very worried.

"It must be hard running a big school with over a thousand teenagers in it," said Turnbull.

"I was enjoying it until about six weeks ago," she replied, "then the muggings after school started. Now every pupil and parent lives in fear."

Turnbull looked at her notes. "Is it true that all 20 pupils were mugged in the same way?"

"Yes," she said. "Nothing is stolen from the victims. They are not hurt but they have all blacked out for a while. When they come to, all their hair is shaved off, including their eyebrows, and there is a red streak of paint on their heads. It's the same for boys and girls."

"What do the victims remember about the mugging?" asked Turnbull.

"At first, they remember nothing. Then they start to have dreams. In the dreams they see the faces of the muggers. They are often the faces of classmates," said the head. "But these classmates always have alibis. At the time of the muggings they are in other places, with other people."

"So where do we go from here?" asked Turnbull.

"Let's talk to the victims to see if we can find out some more information," said Parker.

"Can we borrow a classroom for the day?" Turnbull asked the headteacher.

"You can do anything if it helps us to get some answers," said the headteacher. "Pupils are leaving the school. I've lost 50 so far this month."

Parker and Turnbull got ready to interview the victims in a classroom.

"It brings back memories, doesn't it?" said Turnbull. "I used to sit looking out of the window for hours, feeling bored, especially in Maths."

Parker laughed. "I loved every minute of my lessons, especially Maths," he replied.

Sarah was the first mugging victim who came to see them. She told them about her dream. "In my dream, the muggers were singing and clapping. Their eyes were staring. It was as if they weren't human."

"Sarah, in your dream you said that you saw two boys from your class, Gary and Joe. Is that right?" asked Turnbull.

Sarah nodded. "Yes," she said. "But Gary and Joe aren't the kind of pupils who would be muggers. They're geeks."

Turnbull frowned. "What's a geek?" she asked.

Parker helped her out. "Imagine what I was like at school, Agent Turnbull," he said.

"Wimpy and swotty?" said Turnbull.
"Is that a geek?"

Parker smiled. "You've got it, Turnbull," he said.

The two agents questioned all the victims.

Parker looked at his notes and then he had a brainwave.

"Have you noticed something about all the alibis?" he asked.

"No," Turnbull replied. "But I'm sure you are about to tell me."

"All the so-called muggers belong to the Saint John's Youth Club," he said. "They're always at the youth club when the muggings take place."

"Parker, you're right. I can see why you were always top of the class," Turnbull said.

"It always pays to ask the small questions which build up the details," Parker said, a little smugly. "Like the pieces in a jigsaw puzzle."

"Stop telling me how to do my job and get in the car," Turnbull replied. "Let's check out the Saint John's Youth Club and Bob Brown, who runs it."

CHAPTER THREE

Bob Brown showed the two agents around the youth club. There were about 30 young people there. Some of them were reading. Some of them were doing homework.

"We do some religious reading and spend time helping the boys and girls with their homework," said Bob Brown. "Parents just love this place."

"I bet they do," said Turnbull. "Luckily, many of your members were at the youth club when pupils from their school said they got mugged by them."

"I've already told the police everything I know," said Bob Brown, angrily. "Are you saying that I'm lying about my club members? Look at them. Do you really think these kids are going to leave here for ten minutes to go and rob another teenager on the street? Do they look like streetwise robbers?"

Parker nodded his head. "You may be right," he said.

But Agent Turnbull didn't agree. "They may not look like streetwise muggers," she said. "But they don't look normal either. What kind of youth club has its members sitting around reading or doing homework? They usually play sports and games. It's freaky!"

"Well, if you want to call good manners and hard work 'freaky' that is your business, Agent Turnbull," Bob Brown said. "I must ask you to leave. I have nothing more to say to you."

When he was sure that Parker and Turnbull had left, Bob Brown turned to the club members.

"Now that my visitors have gone," he said, "it is time for us to begin our work."

"Yes, Bob," said the group. They followed him silently, their eyes staring straight ahead.

They went down the stairs that led from the youth club to the cellar. Bob Brown locked the door of the cellar after them. On the wall there was a painting lit up by candles. The group stood around it. They began to chant and clap their hands.

"Members of the zombie army," said Bob Brown, "tomorrow is Hallowe'en, night of the dead. Tomorrow, the red devil in the painting will come to life. The red devil is your master and you are his servants. You must do as he commands. Tomorrow at sunset you must bring a sacrifice to the church."

"Yes, master," the boys and girls chanted, louder and louder. They clapped faster and faster.

Bob Brown didn't know that he had been overheard.
The two agents had stopped their car around
the corner and crept back into the youth club.
They had been listening outside the door.

"If I was a parent, I'd tell my son to skip youth club
and play on his computer for as long as he liked,"
said Turnbull.

"Yes, computers do less harm than this," Parker said.

"Do we arrest Bob Brown now or later?" asked
Turnbull.

"Let's find out exactly what's going on. Let's wait
until tomorrow night and see what he's really up to,"
Parker replied.

"But Agent Parker, it sounds like he's planning
to put a young person's life at risk," she said.
"Can we risk waiting until somebody has ended up
as a sacrifice?"

Parker was silent. He was thinking. "Do you want to
ask Commander Watson, in Headquarters, what we
should do?" he asked.

"No way," she replied. "If Watson thinks there's something interesting about this case, he'll stop us working on it."

"Exactly," said Parker. "We're not sure if we can trust our boss. I think we must wait until tomorrow. This could be a case for the 'Extraordinary Files'."

The agents went up to the painting on the wall and shone their torches on it. It was a religious painting that seemed to show devils and angels. To the far left-hand side was a creature dressed in red with black wings.

"That must be the red devil," Parker said.

"Take a photo of the painting, Parker," Turnbull commanded. "We can track it down on the Internet."

CHAPTER FOUR

Parker and Turnbull went back to their office. They worked all through the night. They looked in art history books and on the Internet. Finally, they found a picture of the painting in a book.

"So tomorrow, at Hallowe'en, the red devil will be on the lookout for a new victim?" asked Turnbull.

Parker nodded. "I think that's the plan. A young person will be given as a sacrifice."

"And who will that young person be?" she asked.

"It will probably be one of the muggers' victims," he said. "We'll need to get a good hiding place in that cellar."

It was Hallowe'en. Lots of children were out 'trick or treating', except for the members of St John's Youth Club. Parker and Turnbull watched them arriving at the hall. There were 20 extra members tonight. They were the victims of the muggings. They still had the red mark on their heads. Their eyes were staring straight ahead, as if they were in a dream.

"They're new members of Bob Brown's zombie army," Parker said.

"One of them will be chosen as the Hallowe'en sacrifice," Turnbull said.

"Not while *we're* here," said Parker. "We must put a stop to it."

The two agents hid in the shadows of the cellar.
Bob Brown and the zombies went up to the painting
and bowed in front of it. The zombies began to chant,
"Oooohmm, oooohmm," and clap their hands.

A girl went to the front. It was Sarah!

"Master of the Universe. Dark Lord and Prince.
We, your servants, are here to do as you command,"
said Bob Brown. "We give you Sarah as a Hallowe'en
sacrifice so that you can show yourself to us."

Sarah stepped forward.

35

It was at that moment that the two agents saw him in the shadows. They had met X before and they knew it meant danger. The candles lit up his large glasses.

It was X. He stepped forward towards Bob Brown.
He took off his glasses. The zombie army gasped with
surprise. There were no eyes in his eye sockets!

"We should have known that he would be here," Turnbull whispered to Parker. "What can we do to stop him?"

Parker wasn't listening. He pulled out his gun and tried to shout out, "Stop! Secret Service! Put your hands up!"

But he had no voice.

A blinding white light filled the cellar. Agents Parker and Turnbull fell down onto the floor as the clock struck midnight.

CHAPTER FIVE

When the two agents woke, it was dawn and they could hear the birds singing. There was no sign of Bob Brown and the youth club members. There was no sign of X. There was also no sign of a sacrifice. Turnbull looked for the painting on the wall but that had also gone.

"After All Hallows Eve comes All Saints' Day,"
Parker said. "It's as if good won over evil at midnight.
Everything is back to normal. Nobody is reported
as missing."

A few hours later, they went to have breakfast.

"I don't know about you Parker, but I'm really tired," Turnbull yawned. "Lying on the floor of that cellar hasn't done me any good."

"Nor me," he said. "But what happened? Did we imagine everything last night?"

"How could we have imagined it?" she replied. "We both saw X there."

"But we didn't see anything happen. In fact, nothing seems to have happened at all." said Parker.

"Unless they killed us," joked Turnbull. "And we're not really here anymore. We're just a couple of ghosts."

He smiled. "Stranger things have happened," he said.

"But if I'm a ghost, why does this hot chocolate taste so good?" she said. "And ghosts never feel tired and I'm very tired."

Parker yawned and nodded his head. He'd been a Secret Service agent for so long now, that nothing, repeat nothing, would have surprised him.

"Let's get some kip, Robert," she said. "For once, the case was solved for us. Tomorrow we'll start again."

GLOSSARY OF TERMS

alibi proof of being somewhere else at the time of the crime

brainwave a good idea

dead end leads nowhere

geek a wimp

Hallowe'en All Hallows Eve when the world of the dead and the world of the living are very close

hoodies bullies who wear hooded tops

kip sleep

MI5 government department responsible for national security

mugging an attack

sacrifice offering

Secret Service Government Intelligence Department

skip miss

streetwise savvy

to come to to wake up

trick or treating a prank played at Hallowe'en

zombie a mindless being

QUIZ

1 Who was following Jack?

2 What did the hoodies do to Jack?

3 Where was the school?

4 Which agent loved Maths at school?

5 Who was in charge of the youth club?

6 What did the members of the youth club do there?

7 Where was the painting?

8 What did the zombies have to bring to the cellar?

9 Who was wearing glasses?

10 How did the agents know they hadn't become ghosts?

ABOUT THE AUTHOR

Paul Blum has taught for over 20 years in London inner-city schools.

I wrote The Extraordinary Files for my pupils so they've been tested by some fierce critics (you!). That's why I know you'll enjoy reading them.

I've made the stories edgy in terms of character and content and I've written them using the kind of fast-paced dialogue you'll recognise from television soaps. I hope you'll find The Extraordinary Files an interesting and easy-to-read collection of stories.

ANSWERS TO QUIZ

1 Three hoodies

2 They shaved his hair off and put a red mark on his head

3 London

4 Agent Parker

5 Bob Brown

6 Read books and do homework

7 In the cellar·

8 A sacrifice

9 X

10 They could taste the hot chocolate and they felt tired